Editor's Note

The stories in this book,
    The Three Little Pigs,
    The Three Billy Goats Gruff,
    and The Town Mouse and the Country Mouse,
have been favorites with generations of young children.
The Three Little Pigs *is an old English folk tale that was
first published in 1843; the version in this book is adapted
from the 1892 retelling by Joseph Jacobs.* The Three Billy
Goats Gruff *is an old Norwegian tale that was published
in English in 1908.* The Town Mouse and the Country
Mouse *is an ancient fable by Aesop that was printed in
English as early as 1484.*

    *All three stories are about animals who find their
own true happiness by keeping their wits about them and
thinking problems out.*

The THREE LITTLE PIGS
and Other Nursery Tales

Illustrated by Christopher Santoro

A GOLDEN BOOK • NEW YORK
Western Publishing Company, Inc., Racine, Wisconsin 53404

Library of Congress Catalog Card Number: 85-81155
ISBN 0-307-12800-8 / ISBN 0-307-62800-0 (lib. bdg.)
A B C D E F G H I J

The Three Little Pigs

THERE WAS an old sow with three little pigs, and as she had not enough to keep them, she sent them out to seek their fortune.

The first that went off met a man with a bundle of straw, and said to him, "Please, man, give me that straw to build me a house."

The man did, and the little pig built a house with it.

Presently along came a wolf, who knocked at the door, and said, "Little pig, little pig, let me come in."

To which the pig answered, "Not by the hair of my chinny-chin-chin."

The wolf then answered, "Then I'll huff, and I'll puff, and I'll blow your house in."

So he huffed, and he puffed, and he blew the house in, and ate up the little pig.

The second little pig met a man with a bundle of sticks, and said, "Please, man, give me some of those sticks to build me a house."

The man did, and the little pig built his house.

Then along came the wolf, and said, "Little pig, little pig, let me come in."

"Not by the hair of my chinny-chin-chin."

"Then I'll puff, and I'll huff, and I'll blow your house in."

So he huffed, and he puffed, and he puffed, and he huffed, and at last he blew the house down, and he ate up the little pig.

The third little pig met a man with a load of bricks, and said, "Please, man, give me those bricks to build me a house."

So the man gave him the bricks, and he built his house with them.

So the wolf came, as he did to the other little pigs, and said, "Little pig, little pig, let me come in."

"Not by the hair of my chinny-chin-chin."

"Then I'll huff, and I'll puff, and I'll blow your house in."

Well, he huffed, and he puffed, and he huffed, and he puffed, but he could *not* get the house down.

When he found that he could not, with all his huffing and puffing, blow the house down, he said, "Little pig, I know where there is a nice field of turnips."

"Where?" said the little pig.

"Oh, in Mr. Smith's field. And if you will be ready tomorrow morning, I will call for you, and we will go together and get some for dinner."

"Very well," said the little pig. "I will be ready. What time do you mean to go?"

"Oh, at six o'clock."

Well, the little pig got up at five and got the turnips
before the wolf came and said, "Little pig, are you ready?"
The little pig said, "Ready! I have been and come back
again and got a nice potful for dinner."

The wolf felt very angry at this, but thought that he
could outsmart the little pig somehow or other, so he said,
"Little pig, I know where there is a nice apple tree."

"Where?" said the pig.

"Down at Merry-Garden," replied the wolf. "And if
you will not deceive me, I will come for you at five o'clock
tomorrow and get some apples."

Well, the little pig bustled up the next morning at four o'clock, and went off for the apples, hoping to get back before the wolf came. But he had far to go and had to climb the tree, so that just as he was coming down from it, he saw the wolf coming, which, as you may suppose, frightened him very much.

When the wolf came up he said, "What, little pig! Are
you here before me? Are they nice apples?"

"Yes, very," said the little pig. "I will throw you
down one."

And he threw it so far that, while the wolf went to pick
it up, the little pig jumped down and ran home.

The next day the wolf came again, and said to the little
pig, "Little pig, there is a fair at Shanklin this afternoon.
Will you go?"

"Oh, yes," said the pig. "I will go. What time shall you
be ready?"

"At three," said the wolf.

So the little pig went off before the time, as usual, and got to the fair and bought a butter churn. He was going home with the churn when he saw the wolf coming. Then he could not tell what to do. So he got into the churn to hide, and by so doing turned it round, and it rolled down the hill with the pig in it, which frightened the wolf so much that he ran home without going to the fair.

He went to the little pig's house and told him how frightened he had been by a great round thing that came down the hill past him.

Then the little pig said, "I frightened you then. I had been to the fair and bought a butter churn. And when I saw you, I got into it, and rolled down the hill."

The wolf was very angry indeed, and declared he would eat up the little pig, and that he would get down the chimney after him.

When the little pig saw what he was doing, he filled his
biggest pot full of water and hung it over the fire. Then,
just as the wolf was coming down, he took off the cover.
The wolf fell into the boiling water, and that was the end
of him. And the little pig lived happily ever afterwards.

The Three Billy Goats Gruff

ONCE UPON A TIME there were three Billy Goats Gruff
who lived on a hillside next to a wide, deep stream.
On the other side of the stream was a field of sweet,
green grass.

Every day the three Billy Goats Gruff looked hungrily at
the field on the other side of the stream. Every day they
longed to eat some of the sweet, green grass.

But to get to the other side of the stream, they had to
cross a wooden bridge. And under the bridge lived a
horrible, mean troll.

One day the littlest Billy Goat Gruff said, "I cannot wait any longer. I am going to cross the bridge and eat the sweet, green grass."

"We will come, too," said his brothers. "We will be right behind you."

Little Billy Goat Gruff started across the bridge. *Trip-trap, trip-trap* went his little hoofs on the planks of wood.

"Who is that *trip-trapping* over my bridge?" said the troll.

"It is I, Little Billy Goat Gruff," said Little Billy Goat Gruff in his wee, small voice.

"I am coming up to eat you!" roared the troll.

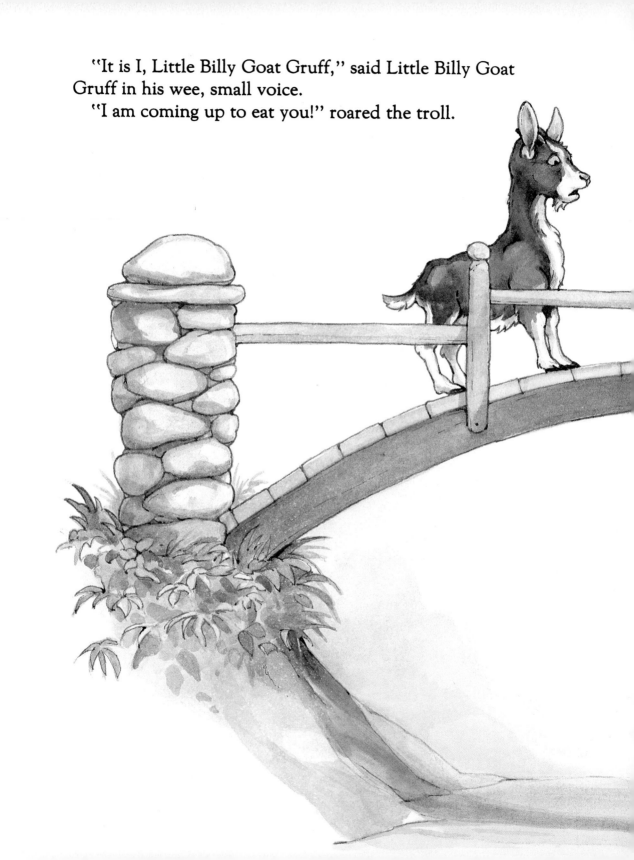

Little Billy Goat Gruff was afraid. "Oh, please don't eat me," he said. "Wait for my big brother. He is much larger and tastier than I am."

"Very well," said the troll, licking his lips. "You may go ahead."

So Little Billy Goat Gruff crossed the bridge and got to the field on the other side.

Then Middle Billy Goat Gruff started across the bridge. *Trip-trap, trip-trap* went his middle-sized hoofs on the planks of wood.

"Who is that *trip-trapping* over my bridge?" called the troll.

"It is I, Middle Billy Goat Gruff," said Middle Billy Goat Gruff in his middle-sized voice.

"I am coming up to eat you!" roared the troll.

Middle Billy Goat Gruff was afraid. "Please don't eat
me," he said. "Wait for my big brother. He is much larger
and tastier than I."

"Very well," said the troll, thinking of the fine meal he
would have. "You may go ahead."

So Middle Billy Goat Gruff crossed the bridge safely
and got to the field on the other side.

Then Big Billy Goat Gruff started across the bridge.
TRIP-TRAP, TRIP-TRAP went his big hoofs on the planks
of wood. The whole bridge shook with his weight.

"Who is that *TRIP-TRAPPING* over my bridge?"
roared the troll in his loudest voice.

"It is I, Big Billy Goat Gruff," shouted Big Billy Goat
Gruff in *his* loudest voice.

"I suppose you are going to tell me to wait for your big
brother," said the troll.

"Oh, no," said Big Billy Goat Gruff. "I am the biggest
one there is."

"Then I am coming up to eat you!" the troll shouted. And he climbed onto the bridge.

Big Billy Goat Gruff was not afraid. "I would like to see you try!" he said.

He rushed at the troll and butted him with his horns. The troll fell off the bridge and disappeared, leaving no trace.

After that the three Billy Goats Gruff crossed the bridge whenever they liked and ate their fill of sweet, green grass.

And the horrible, mean troll never bothered them again.

The Town Mouse and the Country Mouse

A COUNTRY MOUSE was glad to hear that his cousin, the town mouse, was coming to dinner. He gave his cousin all the best food he had—dried beans, peas, and crusts of bread. The town mouse tried not to show how he disliked the food, and picked a little here and tasted a little there to be polite.

After dinner, he said, "How can you stand such food all the time? I suppose here in the country you don't know about anything better. Why don't you come home with me? When you have once tasted the delicious things I eat, you will never want to come back here."

The country mouse not only forgave the town mouse for disliking his dinner, but even consented to go that very evening to the city. They arrived late at night, and the town mouse took his country cousin at once to a room where there had been a big dinner.

"You are tired," he said. "Rest here, and I'll bring you some real food." And he brought the country mouse such things as nuts, dates, cake, and fruit.

The country mouse thought it was all so good that he
wanted to stay there. But before he had a chance to say so,
he heard a terrible roar, and looking up, he saw a huge
creature dash into the room. Frightened out of his wits,
the country mouse ran from the table, round and round
the room, looking for a hiding place.

At last he found a safe place. While he stood there trembling, he made up his mind to go home as soon as he could get safely away. For he said to himself, "I would rather have plain food in safety than dates and nuts in the midst of danger."

Home Sweet Home